The Yellow Belt

Story by Carmel Reilly
Illustrations by Victor McLindon

Contents

Chapter 1	The First Test	2
Chapter 2	A Big Jacket	6
Chapter 3	Very Long Sleeves!	10
Chapter 4	Keep on Moving	14

Chapter 1

The First Test

Noah couldn't wait
to get to his karate class.

Today, he was having his first test.

Noah was a beginner,
so he had a white belt.
If he did well in his test,
he would move up to the next level.
Then he could wear a yellow belt.

Mum and Noah walked into the gym.

"It's time to put your karate jacket on, Noah," said Mum.
"The test will begin soon."

Noah looked in his bag.
But his jacket was not there.

"Oh, no!" he cried. "I can't do the test if I don't have a jacket!"

Karate Belts

Chapter 2

A Big Jacket

A girl was standing near Mum and Noah.

"I have a jacket that you can wear,"
she said to Noah.

She opened her bag
and pulled out a new white jacket.

"Won't it be too big for me?" asked Noah.

"Not if we push up the sleeves," said Mum.

Noah put the jacket on.

"This is enormous," he said.

"Wait," said Mum. "It will be better when I have tied up your belt."

"I look silly!" said Noah.

"Just remember to do all your moves," said the girl.
"You will be all right."

Chapter 3

Very Long Sleeves!

Noah got into line
with the other children.

“Move number one!”
called the teacher.

The children in the line took a step
and held out their left arms.

Noah put his arm out, too.
But his sleeve slipped down.

“Two!” called the teacher.

The children took another step
and held out their right arms.
But Noah didn’t move.
He was trying to push his sleeve up.

“Three!” called the teacher.

Noah saw the other children
begin to move again.

He didn't have time to fix his sleeve.
He needed to catch up!

Chapter 4

Keep on Moving

Noah took a step and held his arm out.
His sleeve fell down again.
But this time,
he didn't push it back up.

Noah kept on moving.
He was not going to let his sleeves
get in the way!

"You were great," said the girl,
when the test was over.

"Thanks," said Noah.
"I have a yellow belt!
And I can't wait for my next class."